PEANUTS®
Shoot for the Moon, SNOOPY!

By Charles M. Schulz

Written by Jason Cooper
Illustrated by Vicki Scott

SIMON SPOTLIGHT

New York   London   Toronto   Sydney   New Delhi

SIMON SPOTLIGHT
An imprint of Simon & Schuster Children's Publishing Division
1230 Avenue of the Americas, New York, New York 10020
This Simon Spotlight edition June 2019
© 2019 Peanuts Worldwide LLC
SIMON SPOTLIGHT and colophon are registered trademarks of Simon & Schuster, Inc.
Manufactured in China 0719 SCP
1 2 3 4 5 6 7 8 9 10
ISBN 978-1-5344-5472-9
This special edition was printed for Kohl's Department Stores, Inc.
(for distribution on behalf of Kohl's Cares, LLC, its wholly owned subsidiary),
by Simon & Schuster, New York.

Kohl's
Style: 54729
Factory: 123386
Production Date: 07/2019

One fine morning Snoopy sat on his doghouse reading an astronaut training book for dogs. NASA was sending astronauts to the moon again, and he was determined to be one of them. *I was the first beagle on the moon,* he thought. *I'll be the second one too!*

Charlie Brown walked by. "If you want to fit into your space suit, Snoopy, you'd better start training!" he said.

Charlie Brown was right! Snoopy headed straight to the park for training . . . after grabbing a snack, of course.

Snoopy stood under a tree warming up for his exercises. He stretched slowly to the right, gradually to the left, then back to the right. In between stretches he enjoyed bites of a giant sandwich. *This sure beats the freeze-dried dog food they'll serve on the spaceship,* he thought.

DESTINATION MOON

Peppermint Patty and Marcie were also at the park. "Look, sir, Snoopy is exercising under that tree," Marcie said. "And he's got a giant sandwich!"
Peppermint Patty jumped down from her swing and said, "Well, I'm curious and hungry! Let's go see what he's up to."

"Hi, Snoopy, nice sandwich," Peppermint Patty said.

"And nice to see you," Marcie added.

Snoopy showed them his astronaut training book and then pointed to a headline in the newspaper. "'NASA Preparing to Blast Off to the Moon and Beyond,'" Marcie read aloud.

Snoopy smiled proudly. *They're looking for a few good beagles!*

"You're going to space?" Peppermint Patty exclaimed. "I could use a visual aid for my science report next week. Do you think you could bring back a moon rock?"

Snoopy nodded.

"Thanks," Peppermint Patty said. "If a real moon rock won't earn me a C+, I don't know what will!"

Peppermint Patty leaned over Marcie's shoulder. "The mission starts tomorrow?" Peppermint Patty said. "Good grief, Snoopy! It takes years of intense work to go to the moon. You need to get into 'spaceship shape' right away. And we're going to help!"

"We don't have enough time, sir!" Marcie protested.

"Don't call me 'sir'!" Peppermint Patty roared. "Call me 'coach'!"

Then Peppermint Patty turned to Snoopy.

"We're going to help you train! We'll show the world you've got the right stuff!"

"You can be quite motivating when you want to be, Sir Coach!" Marcie said.

Does this mean I can't finish my sandwich? Snoopy wondered.

Marcie flipped through Snoopy's book. "Since liftoff is tomorrow, we'll assume you know the math required for your mission. I hope you've calculated the correct distance and speed that you'll need to break out of Earth's atmosphere!"

Yes, of course, Snoopy thought. *I can also confirm that, regrettably, the moon is not actually made of cheese.*

"Then let's start with some intense physical activity," Peppermint Patty declared. "Do twenty jumping jacks and run three laps around the park!"

Snoopy groaned. That sounded a bit *too* intense.

"It's important to exercise in space," Marcie said. "The low gravity affects your muscles, so you need to use them to stay healthy."

Snoopy still wasn't convinced.
Then Marcie said, "Besides, after a workout, you can treat yourself to freeze-dried ice cream!"
Now Snoopy was convinced!

It took a while, but Snoopy finished his workout regimen. Marcie was surprised.
"The fact that you're a beagle and can do one jumping jack is impressive!"
"She's right. Great work," Peppermint Patty said, patting Snoopy on the back.
"You've earned a little break."
Snoopy immediately lay down to take a nap.

After a while Peppermint Patty woke up Snoopy. "Get up, ol' pal! I'm going to show you what it's like to move in a low-gravity environment."

Snoopy was confused. *I thought napping was a low-gravity environment!*

"Gravity is the force that holds your feet on the ground," Marcie explained. "The moon has less gravity than the earth, which means you'll float around like a balloon filled with helium."

Peppermint Patty agreed. "But don't worry, it won't make your voice sound funny."

"Here, Snoopy, I'll demonstrate!"

Peppermint Patty plopped Snoopy down on one end of a seesaw. He was immediately suspicious.

"I'm going to jump on the other end of this seesaw and *launch* you right up into the air!" Peppermint Patty said. "As you're falling, you'll get an idea of what it's like when gravity isn't holding you down. Isn't that clever?"

Snoopy did not think it was clever.

"Sir Coach," Marcie said, "I have another idea. Why don't we use the fountain?"

Peppermint Patty was confused. "A fountain? We're not throwing pennies and making wishes! And stop calling me 'Sir Coach'!"

Marcie explained that Snoopy could float in the water. He would learn what it feels like to move around while his feet aren't touching the ground.

Peppermint Patty sighed. "We can try it, I guess. But it's not as exciting as my seesaw idea."

Inside the fountain Snoopy floated on his back. He glided around by moving his arms up and down.

"How does that feel?" Peppermint Patty asked. "Do you feel lighter than air?"

Snoopy shrugged and thought, *It feels like I'm in a giant birdbath. Don't tell Woodstock, though. I wouldn't want him to get jealous.*

"The last thing we need to do, Sir Coach, is show Snoopy what it's like to walk on the moon," Marcie said. "According to the book, the surface of the moon is covered in craters, rocks, and a lot of dust."

Peppermint Patty paused to think. "Hmm . . . we may need to go to Pigpen's place for this training."

Marcie presented an easier solution. "How about we try the sandbox instead?"

Snoopy stepped into the sandbox. He took a small step, and the sand crunched beneath his feet.

"Just imagine you're on the moon," Peppermint Patty said. "You're in space surrounded by stars. How do you feel?"

Snoopy smiled and thought, *I feel . . . like I've got so much more to explore. . . .*

Snoopy climbed out of the sandbox.

"Well, Snoopy, Marcie and I have done our best to train you! All you need now is a rocket!" Peppermint Patty said.

Snoopy was exhausted but proud. His training was complete. *Excellent,* he thought. *Now I can finish my sandwich!*

Peppermint Patty and Marcie walked Snoopy home. "We're proud of you, Snoopy," Peppermint Patty said. "You learned a lot and you never gave up." Snoopy smiled. *I couldn't have done it without you . . . Sir Coach!*

Charlie Brown was surprised to see Peppermint Patty and Marcie. "What are you two doing here?" he asked.

"We've been training Snoopy for his mission to the moon!" Marcie announced.

"Mission to the moon?" Charlie Brown repeated.

"Of course, Chuck!" Peppermint Patty said. "Don't you read the newspapers?"

"I wonder if he will really make it to the moon," Charlie Brown said.

Suddenly, Snoopy leaped out from behind his doghouse wearing a brand-new space suit. *Ta-da!*

They all laughed.

"I think he's going to try!" said Marcie.

"If any beagle can do it, it's Snoopy!" agreed Peppermint Patty.

Snoopy proudly held up his head. *Here's the world-famous astronaut blasting off for the moon!*